E-MAILS FROM A MADMAN

E-MAILS FROM A MADMAN

namdam a morf sliame

Jarod O. Kintz

iUniverse, Inc.
New York Lincoln Shanghai

E-mails from a Madman
namdam a morf sliame

Copyright © 2006 by Jarod Kintz

All rights reserved. No part of this book may be used or reproduced by any means, graphic, electronic, or mechanical, including photocopying, recording, taping or by any information storage retrieval system without the written permission of the publisher except in the case of brief quotations embodied in critical articles and reviews.

iUniverse books may be ordered through booksellers or by contacting:

iUniverse
2021 Pine Lake Road, Suite 100
Lincoln, NE 68512
www.iuniverse.com
1-800-Authors (1-800-288-4677)

ISBN-13: 978-0-595-39721-1 (pbk)
ISBN-13: 978-0-595-84129-5 (ebk)
ISBN-10: 0-595-39721-2 (pbk)
ISBN-10: 0-595-84129-5 (ebk)

Printed in the United States of America

This book is dedicated to Charles Manseur Fizzlebush Grissham, a.k.a. Mr. Fizzlebush.

20

Dear Guinness Book of World Records,

I am saddened that my proposal to be the first man to swim with his cat in an Olympic-sized swimming pool filled with chocolate milk and Cocoa Puffs has been denied. Oh well, such is life. But I am not deterred. I am on a quest—a quest for a Guinness World Record, and it is my destiny!

I have another proposal for you. I am seeking an answer to the age-old question: how many sixteen-pound bowling balls can be stacked, one on top of another, on the spine of an eight-pound cat? My guess is seven, but I will attempt nine. For the part of the cat, I am using Mr. Fizzlebush, who has a stronger spine than any mammal or marsupial since Frederick the Zildabeest (although Frederick was suspected of using steroids). As his trainer, I assure you that Mr. Fizzlebush is completely natural.

I look forward to hearing from you soon.

Thank you,

Jarod Kintz

8

Dear Disney Cruise Line,

I would very much like to go on one of your cruises, but I have certain accommodations that need to be made before I book my trip. I need a room large enough to comfortably fit a king-size bed, as well as a king (Juan Carlos of Spain).

Juan is afraid of people and will only come aboard incognito. He will be arriving in the costume of a small cat and answers to the pseudonym of "Mr. Fizzlebush." He will need his litter box changed daily, the finest dry cat food, and fourteen bottles of your finest champagne (he is royalty, after all). His Majesty Juan Carlos is not to be touched, but should he decide to lick a crew member's face, he or she will be expected to kneel and grovel at His Majesty's paws. I hope you won't turn your back on a royal customer.

We look forward to sailing with you soon.

Thank you,

Jarod Kintz

5

Dear Dean Silbey,

I have long been a fan of MIT. You guys do amazing work in the field of science. But the reason I am writing today is because I am very concerned about something, and I was hoping you could help me out. I recently moved from Texas to Florida. As you know, there is a two-hour shift in time zones. As I was flying over here, I couldn't stop thinking about those lost two hours.

Where did they go? Did I lose those two hours off my lifespan? Because of my panic, I have temporarily stopped smoking for two days in the hopes of gaining back those lost two hours off my life. I guess my question is, aside from my immediate action, how can I get those lost two hours back? I don't want to die any earlier than I have to (unless I am eating dinner with the in-laws).

I hope to hear back from you soon.

Thank you,

Jarod Kintz

13

Dear NASA,

I am a big fan of space. I really like how there is so much of it. It really makes me feel small and insignificant (although I am, standing only four foot seven) when I really think about it.

My grandpa Melvin was a cheese farmer in Wisconsin. He said the moon is made of cheese. I was wondering, since you've been there, what kind of cheese is it made of? Are there any plans to bring some of this cheese back to earth to sell? I have an idea for a trailer, like the ones that are hooked up on the back of pickup trucks, which you could use to bring some of the cheese back. The trailer would be lined with tinfoil to keep out the radiation and stop the cheese from melting as you reenter the earth's atmosphere.

I hope to hear back from you soon.

Your loyal fan,

Jarod Kintz

PS: I think you should let me fly a shuttle, since I have a terrific driving record. And mother says I can drive a stick like no other child she has (and she has dozens of children).

25

Dear John Howard,

When my Grandma Owen died last month, she left me a sizeable fortune—$13,346.96, to be exact. When I first got the money, I didn't know what to do. My first instinct was to blow it all on a new tricycle. But I stopped myself and thought it would be wiser to invest it. I also knew I wanted to own an island.

This is where you come in. With my inheritance I have purchased two slushies and 652 twenty-dollar Outback Steakhouse gift certificates. So I am offering you 650 gift certificates for your beautiful island of Australia, and I will even let you remain the prime minister once I am crowned.

Please get back to me soon, as I might want to go grab some lunch and be tempted to use the funds otherwise set aside for you.

Sincerely,

Jarod Kintz

20

Dear Yellowstone National Park Visitor Satisfaction Center staff,

I have always loved camping, ever since I was eight, and was forcibly stuffed in a trunk and dropped off in the middle of the forest. My dad was a complex man, but I believe he was trying to show me the value of camping. In the spirit of my father, I will be enlightening my neighbor to the joys of camping. (Currently, he's hog-tied in my basement.) Anyway, I just wanted to make sure that you take as good of care of him as you did of me all those years ago.

Your Fellow Camper,

Jarod Kintz

8

Dear Chick-fil-A,

My grandmother Mildred recently died a most gruesome death, and in her passing, I was left with her chicken farm empire. I have about three hundred chickens that I have no use for—with the exception of Larry, my childhood chicken friend.

I want to sell you the chickens, at cutthroat prices (no pun intended). Do I have to cut the head off of each chicken before I ship them, or just stuff them whole into boxes? I would be willing to sell each for ten dollars, and I might even be willing to let Larry go for twenty dollars, seeing as how he was always such a loyal friend.

Let me know quickly, as I need the cash.

Best,

Jarod Kintz

9

Dear Ringling Brothers,

The circus has always been like a second home to me, even though I have no first home.

That's right, I'm homeless. Living in the streets has allowed for some unique ways to pass the time. Out of extreme hunger I have learned how to swallow my arm up to my elbow, bunch up my fist, and fool my stomach into thinking it's full. I usually sleep like this, but sometimes my arm goes numb and I have to pull it out.

This is where you come in. Recently, I told my friend that I wanted to join the circus, and s/he (I think the technical term is *hermaphrodite*) laughed at me. Nevertheless, I am willing to swallow my pride, as well as my arm, on a nightly basis in return for a warm meal and a chance to see the world. I currently have no address to which you can reply, so I'm going to assume you will accept my offer, and I'll just show up at your tent.

Thank you,

Jarod Kintz

3

Dear Makestickers.com,

I am the proud owner of a bumper sticker, but I don't know how to use it. It didn't come with a bumper, and I was wondering if you could tell me where I might be able to buy a bumper?

Thanks,

Jarod Kintz

1

Dear McDonald's,

Yesterday, while eating a cheeseburger, I bit into something funny. When I looked down I saw that along with the cheeseburger, there was the tip of someone's finger. Then I noticed that I myself was missing the tip of my finger, and I was bleeding quite profusely.

My appetite was momentarily spoiled, so I returned my cheeseburger for a full refund. But in my carelessness, I accidentally returned the tip of my finger, as well. I was wondering how to go about getting that missing piece from my life known as my fingertip, since I need it really badly. (How else am I supposed to get way in the back of my nose when picking it?)

I'm not pointing my finger at you, because this is entirely my fault. I would just like it back. I look forward to hearing from you.

Yours Truly,

Jarod Kintz

12

Dear Victoria's Secret,

I understand that you make sexy underwear and bras. Is this true? If so, I have some ideas I'd like to share with you.

Have you ever thought about making bras out of recycled cans? They wouldn't be as comfy for sure, but they'd definitely be more environmentally friendly. And as we all know, boobies are the most environmentally friendly thing known to man.

Also, have you ever thought about expanding into the hat industry? You could make hats out of panties, for all of us guys who like to wear our girlfriends' panties on our heads.

These are just a few of the ideas I have. We can arrange a meeting to discuss the others. I look forward to your reply.

Sincerely,

Jarod Kintz

13

Dear Fruit of the Loom,

I have a question for you that concerns the nutritional value of undergarments.

How many homeless people could survive a week by eating a package of your underwear? My guess is four, but my friend Mr. Fizzlebush thinks seven can survive. Which of us is right? And what kind of fruit are your underwear made out of? To me it tastes like apples, but Mr. Fizzlebush thinks they taste like raisins. Again, which of us is correct?

I hope to hear back from you soon.

Best,

Jarod Kintz

18.

Dear Snapple,

How do I get to be on your commercials? I'm a huge fan of Snapple, especially your bottles. I like how the lid goes clickity-click-click-click when I push it in really fast with my thumb. Oh yeah, and it tastes swell, too.

Well, I've said some pretty nice things about you. Now it's your turn to say some pretty nice things about me.

Sincerely,

Jarod Kintz

2

Dear Holiday Inn,

Summer is coming up, and that means travel is going to be up, also.

In considering the hotel industry, a problem occurred to me. People have to come to you. Why don't you go to the people? Or, more specifically, *with* the people? Yes, I'm talking about a portable hotel. I don't know how you would do this, but you guys aren't keeping up with the times. Computer chips keep getting smaller and smaller, yet your rooms are still in the twentieth century. If you could make your rooms the size of a penny, people could start vacationing in their own sofa cushions. A whole new travel industry would be born.

I hope you guys take this thought seriously, and I look forward to staying in a hotel room in my pocket.

Sleep well,

Jarod Kintz

15

Dear Nike,

It has just come to my attention that you make shoes. It might have come to my attention earlier if I was someone who wears shoes. But I only wear gloves, because I was born with hands for feet. So when I meet new people, I don't shake their hand; I just sort of tickle their feet.

I am interested in getting into marathons, and I was wondering if you could design a special glove for me that had air on the bottom, because my hand-feet get so blistered and sore. Also, since you guys are the kings of sports, if I am playing soccer, can I pick the ball up with my hand-feet and throw it without getting penalized? It would be like Pele meets Jordan meets Mark Twain (people tell me I look just like him).

I'd love it if we could meet. So many people to meet, and so many feet to greet. (That's a little joke my mom tells me when I get depressed about my nonconformity.) I guess you could say I have the ultimate foot fetish. People are always obsessed with things that they don't have, right? Oh boy, if I had a wife for every hand I have, I'd be a Mormon.

Anyway, it was good writing to you, and I look forward to hearing back from you.

Best,

Jarod Kintz

15

Dear Amazon.com,

Winter always reminds me of warm fires, but it's been several years since I've burned a forest down. I like your site, but I didn't see where to buy any trees.

If I were a tree, I'd probably be the Joshua Tree, even though my name is Jarod. I have a cousin named Josh, but he's not a tree…although he moves about as much as a tree (he has no legs).

Do you sell exotic animals on your Web site? Do you think pythons would make good babysitters?

Tell me when you get some trees in stock, or exotic snakes, or both. I can hardly wait for your reply.

Thank you,

Jarod Kintz

9

Dear History Channel,

Your channel is the only channel on TV that's worth watching. Well, besides the Discovery Channel. And the Learning Channel. Oh, and Comedy Central and HBO. And let's not forget ESPN and FUSE. But aside from those, I only watch your channel. Except for some of the shows on Bravo or USA.

And although I don't work out, I'm kind of a history buff, and I want to start a reality show on your channel on which I interview all the big names in history. Names like Jesus, Caesar, Alexander the Great, and Rob Pilatus from Milli Vanilli.

I've already got pertinent interview questions lined up—questions like, "Alex, your full name is Alexander the Great, right? How does it feel to have a definite article, or function word, for a middle name? Was your father's middle name 'the' as well?" And also, "Rob (of Milli Vanilli), musically, you're a prodigy. Some say Mozart was the most brilliant musician who ever lived, but you were unequivocally the greatest lip-syncher who's ever lived. That's a notch up from being the best air guitarist of all time. How does it feel to have been the top in your chosen vocation? Now Rob, I hear you answering these questions, but how do I know that you are really answering these questions, and your replies are not just playing on a prerecorded CD?"

So you can see that I've got the important questions for the important people. I'll provide the questions, but I'll need you to provide the transportation (the time machine). And if you don't already have one, and it gets invented in, say, five hundred years or so, just swing back through this era and pick me up and let me do the show. You'll already be going in my direction anyway—might as well stop and dig me up.

Best,

Jarod Kintz

19

Dear Bicycle Playing Cards,

Hi, my name is Jarod, and my knees are bleeding. It's really hard to ride a bicycle and play solitaire at the same time. I once played a game of speed going well over twenty miles an hour. But I was too involved in the game to see the oncoming traffic, and I nearly ran over Old Man Willard. (Don't worry, he's already in a wheelchair.)

But the reason I am writing you today is I am trying to learn how to play No Limit Texas Hold 'Em. Are there any tips you could give me to improve my game? Lots of people wear sunglasses while they play, but I think I am going to wear a helmet. Do you think that will help me out? Like a beaver, I eagerly await your reply.

Thank you,

Jarod Kintz

20

Dear Chanel,

First let me start by saying that I am not confused about my sexuality, but I just LOVE wearing your perfume. I don't know which of your scents is my favorite, but I have a suggestion for you. I feel the scent of mothballs is underrated in today's society. When I become the world's greatest grandmother (God willing), I will unleash a powerful new fragrance. I'll call it "Grandmother's House." Old men will love it, and little children will fear it. I want you to bottle it and distribute it for me.

We'll work out my percentage later. Just ponder the merits of mothballs and get back to me. This makes good scents.

Thank you,

Jarod Kintz

8

Dear John Deere,

I think your tractors are sexy. I also think the way freshly cut grass smells is sexy, although not when you stuff a bunch of it up your nose. Cows eat grass, and people eat cows, but can people also eat grass? I know I do, but mother only lets me eat it after I've finished everything on my plate at the dinner table. Then she'll let me into the yard so I can munch on it until I throw up (just like the cows do).

Why is your mascot a deer? I think it should be a cow. John Cow. It sounds more prestigious. Cows are a case study in elegance (when they're not eating their own vomit, that is). Lots of people worship cows, but hardly anyone worships deer. Maybe, if you change your mascot to a cow, you could have over one billion people in India worshiping your tractors the same way I do. Just a thought.

Let me know what you think about my cow concept.

Sincerely,

Jarod Kintz

5

Dear Apple Computers,

Hello, my name is Jarod, and I am going to open up a computer company very shortly (as soon as grandmother gives me the go-ahead). But don't worry, I won't be taking away any of your market share. That's because my company will be called Orange Computers. Apple Computers and Orange Computers—they're not compatible! So that's good news for you, Steven, or whoever is reading this.

But maybe someday we can merge companies and become the Dole beverages of the computer industry. Or maybe not, because apple juice makes me wheeze and vomit in other people's shoes. Well, it was great chatting to you, Steven. Gotta go, I think I hear the garage door opening. (I hope grandmother's not drunk again.)

Take Care,

Jarod Kintz

19

Dear Ford,

I think my Ford Explorer door is broken. It just won't close. I think this is because I don't have the rest of the Explorer, I only have the door.

It's a passenger-side door, and I bought it from a passenger. Also, it doesn't seem to be able to lock. I think the latch isn't catching, or something.

I think it's missing some crucial parts, and I'd like to order them from you. I need: one frame, four wheels, a body, another door, an engine, a steering wheel, and some of those air fresheners that you stick in the vents. And I'm feeling frisky with my money, so let me go ahead and order some brakes while I'm at it. You can send the bill to the Pizza Hut on San Jose Boulevard. They'll just deliver it to me, along with the pizza I just ordered.

Thank you,

Jarod Kintz

8

Dear Hair Cuttery,

I am pleased to inform you that I will be bringing a special boy to your store for his first haircut. Yay!

Mr. Fizzlebush is finally turning four, and I figured it was time that he get a haircut. I want you to shave the sides, leave the top long, and gel it up in a Mohawk. I think he'll look adorable. We might have a problem getting him to sit still, though. He has tons of energy!

What usually works to get him to lie down is to rub his belly, or at the base of his spine. He loves that. But don't worry, Mr. Fizzlebush doesn't bite. In fact, he might even lick you, or himself, while you are trying to cut his hair.

I look forward to our first trip to the haircutters, and I'll see you then.

Best,

Jarod Kintz

1

Dear Crayola,

You have so many beautiful colors among your crayon selection that, if someone forced me to either choose my favorite Crayola crayon color or snort a bottle of glue, I'd be forced to snort the glue. Have you ever super glued your upper lip to your nose?

Do you know what the world record for the most consecutive crayons shoved up one's own nostril is? I'm trying to get a world record. I once stuck gum in Mr. Fizzle bush's hair, and he didn't talk to me for a week. But then I let him use my Crayola crayons and he forgave me. So, I'm just writing to tell you that you saved our friendship. Hey, that could be your new slogan: "Crayola builds friendships, and is healthier than snorting glue."

You can have it. It's a gift. You helped me, so it's the least I can do. Let me know if you like it.

Best,

Jarod Kintz

4

Dear American Psychological Association,

I consider conversations with people to be mind exercises, but I don't want to pull a muscle, so I stretch a lot. That's why I'm constantly either rolling my eyes or yawning. But yesterday, I had a rather extensive phone conversation with a girl (well over five minutes) without limbering up first, and today my brain is so stiff and sore that I can't seem to think about anything except what shade her nipples might be. I think I strained my brain. Or maybe I have a brain cramp.

How do I recover from this? I know potassium helps cramps, but I'm already walking around with a banana in my pocket. What should I do?

Yours truly,

Jarod Kintz

15

Dear Ashley Furniture,

I don't know if you are aware of it or not, but an albino midget with a wooden leg and two metal crutches makes for the world's greatest barstool—unless, of course, he's an alcoholic albino midget with a wooden leg and two metal crutches, because not only is he a liability then, but he'll probably also drink all the alcohol at the bar.

I was wondering if you have any sober stools in stock? I also like them to be wearing those fuzzy, furry Russian hats on their heads because it makes the seating much more comfortable. Can I customize the fabric on the barstool? I really don't like naked furniture, especially on a midget.

I look forward to shopping at your store!

Thank you,

Jarod Kintz

23

Dear Rolex,

I usually don't steal, but I just ripped off a Rolex. It came with the arm I pulled off of Mr. Patel. Never do business in India with a leper.

But the watch works great—a little bulky because the elbow sticks out of my pocket. (He hadn't eaten in weeks, so he was very bony.) I don't know how he got the watch, or the leprosy. Probably the same way we catch a cold over here. I wouldn't mind the sniffles for a nice timepiece such as you make.

So I'm just writing to congratulate you on your superb craftsmanship and elegance of design. I know if Mr. Patel still had his arm, he'd jump up and give you a high five. Well, I'm getting madder by the minute, so I'd better go. Tick tock to you later.

Sincerely,

Jarod Kintz

2

Dear PetSmart,

Every day I take my dogs for a walk in the park. They're not real dogs—rather, they're metaphorical ones. They're my feet, but they are really hairy, they smell horrible, and they have been known to attack old people's faces.

I don't want to put my feet to sleep, but I'm tired of having them prowl around under my neighbor's bedroom window late at night. What should I do? Also, how do I stop my feet from sniffing my crotch? It's embarrassing at corporate functions to be giving a speech and have one foot sniff my goods while the other one scratches my balls.

I look forward to hearing your solution.

Thank you,

Jarod Kintz

5

Dear NASCAR,

I can see why you guys are among the fastest growing sports in America. With all the risk of dependency with sleep medications, you guys fit a nice niche among insomniacs. I'm glad you guys came around—and around—and around. I get so tired of counting sheep, and of all the lustful presleep thoughts that sheep-counting generates. So keep up the good work, and bring on the Zs.

Best,

Jarod Kintz

8

Dear adidas,

Every morning, I wake up glad to be alive. Most people don't have ten things to be thankful for, but I do. I can count my blessings on my fingers and toes.

So every morning I count twenty-four blessings (I have nine toes on my left foot), but owning a comfortable pair of running shoes is not one of them. It's sad that I can play the piano with my feet, but yet it's so painful for me to go jogging with my dog. What's even more tragic is that my dog died from obesity (all he ever did was watch TV and eat sausages.) But I might have been able to save him had I owned a good pair of running shoes.

How much will it cost me to special order a custom pair of shoes? I look forward to your speedy reply.

Thank you,

Jarod Kintz

9

Dear Random House publishing,

Is getting a book published with you guys really a random process? Maybe you guys only publish every other book, or novels that have prime numbers as the total amount of pages. That'd be really random. Or if all your authors were under four feet eleven…

I'm working on putting a book together, but I can't figure out how to glue the pages to the spine. Is this where an agent comes in? How long should my book be? I was thinking sixty-five inches—that's how long my girlfriend is. I want to tattoo the novel all over her body. I think I'd get a lot of men to want to read my book, but I wouldn't let them. I wouldn't even let your editors see my girlfriend's breasts. Well, maybe I will. But no blind editors—this book is not written in Braille.

Let's meet up for lunch and discuss the details further. I'll have my people (they're all under four feet eleven) contact your people.

Sincerely,

Jarod Kintz

14

Dear Irish Spring,

I simply adore the way your soap smells—and the way it tastes.

When I was growing up I had the foulest of mouths. Mother wouldn't wash my mouth out with soap; she'd make me eat the whole bar. I must have eaten at least three bars of Irish Spring every day from the ages four to thirteen. And by then, I wouldn't eat anything else.

I've branched out a little since then. I do eat my vegetables and an occasional deodorant stick, but mainly I still munch on a bar of your soap while I surf the net and enjoy filthy thoughts.

Most people have a shower in the morning and then eat their breakfast. Not me—I have my breakfast while I'm showering. I just wanted to let you know that I will continue consuming your excellent soap as long as you make it. I am a man of dirty thoughts and a clean mouth, thanks to you. And for that, I am fucking grateful.

Sincerely,

Jarod Kintz

4

Dear Movado,

Time…where does it all go?

How do you manage to squeeze all the time in the world into such a tiny watch, yet still keep it sophisticated and uncluttered? Every hour of every day of everyone's life is stuffed inside your watches, and those two hands on the beautiful faces of every Movado are slowly strangling the life out of all of us. But I don't consider you to be a killer. No, you're much too sexy to be a killer. Or maybe I'm just mad and you are out to end my life, one guesstimated minute at a time.

With love,

Jarod Kintz

20

Dear Starbucks,

While I've never actually bought a cup of your coffee, I have had many of them thrown in my face. Some people can be so sensitive about their weight!

Have you ever had a sunburn on your retina? That must be what it feels like to have a steaming hot cup of coffee splashed in your eyes. And what's with your new policy which states that I must wear pants to lounge around in your chairs and engage in small talk with your customers? How many times will I be forcefully thrown out of your stores before I don't come back? Only about twelve more times is all.

And I'd like to tell you that one of your employees didn't wash his hands after using the restroom. I knew those cameras I secretly installed in the bathrooms would come to good use one day.

Sincerely,

Jarod Kintz

8

Dear Mercedes,

Driving a Mercedes has always been a status symbol, much like being a member of a country club. I'm willing to speculate that a Mercedes is a frequently stolen vehicle.

While I don't have a Mercedes, I do have a member of a country club. Actually I have two, but only one of them was stolen. (Not by me, of course. I just picked him up for a great price.) Do you think that if I got a piggyback ride around town from this country club member that I would get as much respect as if I were riding in a Mercedes? Maybe not, but the gas mileage would be better. Well, I'm off to turn some heads with my new ride.

Best,

Jarod Kintz

5

Dear Moe's,

Have you ever wondered…if you were a burrito, what kind you'd be? I have. It's all I ever seem to think about these days.

I wouldn't like to be short and fat, like I am now, or tall and skinny, like I am now, but maybe somewhere in the middle, like I am now. I wouldn't be much to look at, but I'd be a good burrito, and father. It's what's on the inside that counts, right? I guess I'm not a good person or father now, because I'm not full of cheese and beans and sour cream.

Every day I try to better myself by eating a pound of cheese and a pint of sour cream, but I'll never be half the burrito you guys make there at Moe's. You guys, and your burritos, are my inspiration in life.

With love,

Jarod Kintz

12

Dear Myspace.com,

You are my favorite addiction. Oh, I've tried other things too. But the booze, the broads, the coke, meth, heroin, gambling, guns, and *Golden Girls*…they just don't compare to you. It's good to be completely sober yet intoxicated online at all times.

You've ruined my life, but you are also my savior. I'd like to slap you, and then give you a quick high five. Maybe two. Well, I better go, I have a new message. Yay!

Best,

Jarod Kintz

1

Dear Pepsi,

Your scrumptious beverage goes great with just about any meal. The only meal it doesn't go good with is a meal with the in-laws. The only beverage that perfectly accompanies a meal with the in-laws would have to be either hemlock or cyanide.

I like Pepsi better than Coke. In fact, in a recent blindfold taste test conducted by my friends, we discovered that out of three cups, I liked Pepsi the second best. I liked it better than Coke, but not as much as what later turned out to be some strange mixture of bodily fluids and Cheese Whiz. My friends are brilliant culinary artists, and currently work within the food industry. (Who knew fingernail clippings could add so much texture to tacos?)

I believe you also own Taco Bell, and you might want to think about promoting these upstanding chefs.

Yours Truly,

Jarod Kintz

21

Dear Papa John's,

Your pizza crust has to be the best crust on earth. Well, besides the actual crust of the earth, that is. Hey, if all the oceans were pizza sauce, and rain were cheese, I could probably eat my way to Portugal. And if the Portuguese people were olives, I could eat them too.

So I'm thinking of setting up a store called Mama John's. I'd resell pizzas that I'd order from you. I'd lose money at first, but eventually I'd turn a profit. You've been the best pizza place for years, but it's time to have some healthy competition, and who better to put you in your place than your wife? Hope you don't mind.

Best,

Jarod Kintz

7

Dear Suave,

Your hair product smells so divine that sometimes I start crying while thinking about it. I cry because I am bald, and I have no hair to lather up. Never again will I feel your soft shampoo work itself through my hair and engulf my fingers as it used to.

The only time I get to enjoy your shampoo now is at potluck dinners, where I bring a dessert crafted from Suave shampoo. It saddens me that I am the only one who eats it. Nobody wants to eat the dish that the bald man brings. Hey, at least there's no hair in my food, unlike the popular Vanessa and her lasagna, where I always find a stringy hair every time I eat it. I don't think she uses your product, and I can't accept her as a person because of that.

I am thinking of buying wigs—not to wear, but solely to wash every morning in the shower just to have the Suave experience before I start my day.

I just thought I'd let you guys know how much you mean to me. Even though the bald man is probably seen as the enemy at your corporate offices, I am your most committed customer.

Sincerely,

Jarod Kintz

8

Dear American Association of Psychics,

Sometimes I think I can see into the future. It's crazy, but I actually knew during the last sentence what I was going to write in this sentence just seconds before the period came. I'm like that all the time.

I once foresaw my neighbor's house getting vandalized weeks before it happened. Preparation is the key to not getting caught. So is not leaving your pants with your wallet and license in them on the master bedroom floor while you roll around naked on their sheets singing the theme song to Golden Girls. But that's just speculation on my part.

Well, I gotta go, but I'm sure you already knew that.

Good luck in the future,

Jarod Kintz

20

Dear RE/MAX,

Don't get me wrong, I love living here in Florida, but I feel like I need a change.

If I could live anywhere in the world, I'd probably want to live in a vending machine in an abandoned warehouse. My neighbor would be a Kit Kat bar. Would it be weird to want to eat your neighbor?

I couldn't have any dogs, because my chocolate neighbors could kill my dogs if they ate one. I generally don't like it when my dogs eat my neighbors (with the obvious exception of the Wilsons), but in this case, I really wouldn't like it.

If I had a party, would everyone have to pay a dollar to enter my vending-machine neighborhood? It'd be the ultimate gated community. I look forward to your reply.

Sincerely,

Jarod Kintz

5

Dear General Electric,

Back before Edison invented the light bulb, if someone had an idea, did a candle light up above their head?

I'm sure glad that he invented the light bulb, because I have lots of ideas. And most of them occur while huffing gasoline, and gasoline and candles don't mix too well. Not like vodka and orange juice mix, which also helps me generate ideas. Sometimes I drink so much that I lose my balance, which isn't good for business, seeing as I'm a tightrope walker. I just sort of fell into the business after the last guy fell out the business, and into the treacherous depths of Niagara Falls.

It's a fine line to walk when judging how much to drink. I'm sure Edison would have made a great tightrope walker. I always sweat profusely while walking across Niagara Falls. Edison intuitively knew what I go through when he said, "Genius is 99 percent perspiration and 1 percent inspiration." While I may not be a tightrope-walking genius, I do perspire enough to be considered at least brilliant.

The funny thing about my business is, nobody who watches me wants to see me reach the other side. They all want to see me step over the line into a tumultuous, watery grave.

Well, I gotta run now, or rather walk, very, very slowly.

Sincerely,

Jarod Kintz

18.

Dear San Diego Zoo,

I am pleased to announce that on the thirteenth of June, between noon and 12:15 PM, Mr. Fizzlebush and I will be arriving at your magnificent zoo.

Yes, I did say that I was arriving with the legendary Mr. Fizzlebush. Unfortunately, due to time constraints, and the fact that he can't hold a pen in his tiny paws, Mr. Fizzlebush will not be able to sign autographs. But he will be available to take some provocative pictures with the finest felines in your facility. To not create too much of a spectacle in your zoo, both Mr. Fizzlebush and myself will dress covertly. I will be dressed in all green spandex with a giant shell on my back, and Mr. Fizzlebush will be dressed like Humphrey Bogart's piano in *Casablanca*.

Of all the zoos, in all the towns, in all the world, we're coming to yours. On a side note, Mr. Fizzlebush's costume will likely be rented, and probably out of tune and not musical at all, so unfortunately, I won't be able to play a little ditty for you on the piano. See you soon.

Sincerely,

Jarod Kintz

1

Dear Burger King,

It seems that we are on the verge of a fast-food feudal war. You claim to be the burger king, yet it is I who lay rightful claim to the royal throne of all greasy patties, regardless of whether they are thinly disguised by a layer of pseudocheese. We must decide who keeps the title.

We must have a duel, using the most ancient of weapons: a single slice of processed cheese, and no more than two ketchup packets. Meet me behind the dumpster at the San Jose Burger King in Jacksonville, Fla. Like a cheese single, there can be only one. Down with your monarchy of mass-produced hamburgers.

Have a great day,

Jarod Kintz

14

Dear Dannon,

In addition to cutlery, I have always been a connoisseur of spoons, from the contemporary to the ancient. And it is the natural progression of a spoon collector to advance to collecting unopened, mint-condition yogurt containers.

Considering that I just started collecting yogurt containers two years ago, it is mildly remarkable that I now have over forty thousand unopened and out-of-date (this makes them a rarity and increases intrinsic value) yogurt containers.

I was wondering if you were going to come out with a limited edition collector's yogurt container this year? The members of YAYA (Young American Yogurt Association), of which there are two of us—Mr. Fizzlebush and myself—would be willing to pay top dollar to obtain a pallet of them if you were to come out with them.

As a contrarian, I believe you've got to do the opposite of what the masses are doing to be successful, and nobody is investing in yogurt now. Not even the Oracle of Omaha, Warren Buffet, sees the future value of unopened, out-of-date yogurt. I look forward to hearing about the collector's edition yogurt.

Thank you,

Jarod Kintz

4

Dear Planters,

Hello, my name is Jarod, and I am a costume jazz musician. I would like to apply to perform at your next corporate function.

My band's name is Good Elephants Make Good Neighbors. (We all dress in elephant costumes.) Jazz and blues, as you are probably already aware, are born out of sadness. We are method musicians, or we actually submerge ourselves in our characters before every performance. The best thing for a jazz performance would be ultimate sadness and anger.

And what is saddest thing that could happen to an elephant? Well, if that elephant was allergic to peanuts, that would be pretty sad. So my band and I will be playing that day from the perspective that we are depressed and angry that we ate peanuts and we broke out in rashes. And Tommy, the pianist, always takes it a little too far, so it might be helpful if you don't have your peanut mascot present that day.

I look forward to hearing back from you about further booking questions.

Thank you,

Jarod Kintz

12

Dear Prada,

Your handbags are so elegant that they must make women's arms feel like royalty. It must be a sweet feeling walking around with two queens stuck to one's side, and having the aristocracy work for you.

I know if I felt like I had a couple of kings glued to my side, I'd have them fight for territory, and then I'd swoop in and label them as heretics and have them beheaded. Sure, I might have no hands then, but I'd be the moral superior. People should fear the man, and not the hand.

So in a way, your purses make the philosophical claim that democracy is superior to any monarchy. Yet, paradoxically, Prada is the king of purses. So even though your philosophy might be noble, you intellectually undercut yourself by the quality of your product. But you should make light out of this paradox, and create the world's first purse that resembles the head of a famous beheaded queen. Not only will it be a novelty, but it will let people know where you stand on this great social issue.

Let me know what you think of my Mary Queen of Scots, and other famous beheaded royalty, idea for a new line of purses.

Sincerely,

Jarod Kintz

9

Dear Guinness,

This is my third attempt to qualify for a world record. I have a unique talent that might be record-breaking.

Some people, circus people, swallow swords. I don't swallow swords, I shit spoons. And the crazy thing is, I only eat forks. I'm a human silverware factory. So my proposal is to declare myself the most portable and low-overhead factory since the Industrial Revolution. I know that those damned Victorian Brits would have loved to showcase me in a display in a glass house.

So there it is. If that is not record-worthy, I don't know what is. Also, what's the world record for the most rejected Guinness proposals? I look forward to hearing from you.

Thank you,

Jarod Kintz

11

Dear University of Florida,

I think you should change your sports mascot from a gator to the mathematical sign, "greater than," known symbolically as >. Florida State could be the "less than" sign, <, instead of the Seminoles. That way, when you two play, the newspaper headline on the day after the game might read, "Florida Greaters greater than Less Than, but not equal to." Let me know what you think.

Thank you,

Jarod Kintz

5

Dear Hummer,

Nothing could look tougher, yet so ruggedly handsome, than your SUV, not even if someone laid Arnold Schwarzenegger on his stomach, drilled two axles through him, and stuck four wheels on them. If machine became man, I think your automobile could run, and win, to become the first SUV governor of California. It'd be the SUVernor.

Are you planning on running your H3 for president in 2008? If you need a campaign manager, look no further than right here. Not to blow my own horn, but I'm like a self-conscious saxophone marching in a one-man band with no conductor, and no legs to step to. That's how I roll. I look forward to leading your campaign for the presidency.

Sincerely,

Jarod Kintz

1

Dear Gallo,

You guys just might be the greatest modern-day wine makers. If it wasn't for Jesus, you might be the greatest of all time. But you make wine from grapes, and he made it from water. The only thing I can make from water is Kool-Aid, and even then I still need the Kool-Aid mix.

Wine is at least a billion-dollar industry, and if your grapes didn't grow on the vine, you'd actually have money growing on trees. But what if money literally did grow on trees, and I wanted to eat a pile of cash with some friends? Would you recommend a white wine, or a red wine, with that meal? Or what about a pink wine? A blending of the two—pink and green go great together.

Well, good luck with your grapes, and I hope this year, and every year is a good year for your wines.

Best,

Jarod Kintz

12

Dear American Dental Association,

Without dentists, there would be no teeth. And without teeth, there would be no toothpicks. And toothpicks, as you are probably aware, are the greatest invention in the history of man.

One day we're making toothpicks, the next we're landing on the moon. So without dentists, there would be no landing on the moon. And if we didn't land on the moon, the Russians might have won the Cold War. So the dentistry profession single-handedly won us the Cold War.

So no matter what people might say about dentists, you guys are real American heroes in my book—and my book is very short and full of bright pictures and lovely scented flowers that I plucked from my neighbor's garden before laminating them and gluing them on the cover.

Basically, my book is a bunch of pictures of my favorite dentists, and their brief biographies. In fact, the only other person in my book who is a non-dentist patriot is the man with no arms who goes around the neighborhood kicking over everybody's trash cans on trash day. This country was founded by rebels, and in his own little way, he's making a bold political statement. I don't know exactly what he's trying to enlighten us with, but it might have something to do with our current economic situation and ballooning debt. Or maybe he's mad at "the man" for holding the armless man down.

Anyway, if you guys want me to, I'll make some copies of my book so that you can promote it at your next convention. Let me know if you are interested.

Thank you,

Jarod Kintz

12

Dear Uno,

I am your numero Uno fan. I've been playing Uno ever since I was cuatro (four). But I feel it's time to introduce a sequel to your game, an Uno 2 if you will. Or even better, Uno Dos.

Instead of yelling "uno" one card before you go out, you'd yell "uno dos" when you only have tres (three) cards left. Let me know what you think about the sequel to Uno.

Muchas gracias,

Jarod Kintz

19

Dear Six Flags,

If anybody knows about roller coasters (besides you guys, of course), it's me. It's my middle name, or names, as it is two words.

Whatever happened to wooden roller coasters? Today all I see are metal ones. Have you ever considered making a roller coaster out of pencils? You might have shorter lines this way. Or maybe use toothpicks, and have the seats be sandwiches (minus the mayonnaise, of course). It would be the world's fastest sandwich, even though I have been known to hurl a Rueben sandwich at nearly ninety miles per hour.

I'm stoked about sandwiches, so let's put this project into motion, and get roller coasters popping like a brown lunch bag full of air that meets headlong into an open palm.

Sincerely,

Jarod Roller Coaster Kintz

8

Dear Big Lots,

Do you sell log cabins in your store, or just the lots?

Lincoln grew up in a log cabin, but not one of the ones that you should sell in your stores. If tallness is greatness, Lincoln was the greatest president in this country's history by a long shot—well, several inches anyway.

I don't measure greatness by the tallness of things. I measure greatness by widths. In this case, I think your store is superior to Wal-Mart, which has paradoxically the narrowest aisles and the widest customers. I think you should come out with a new slogan that says, "Girth is greatness—and we're the biggest."

Go ahead and take it, I've got many more ideas. If you do decide to use it, however, I'd like to play Lincoln on the commercial. (I'll get shot in the commercial, and that symbolizes shooting down the competition.) I look forward to hearing back from you on this.

Thank you,

Jarod Kintz

1

Dear Parker Brothers,

I feel the decline in board game popularity and the rise in video games among America's youth signals a decline in society.

America's youth have weak minds and strong thumbs. In fact, if thumbs were bodies, I'd be carrying a pair of Arnold Schwarzenegger's, which I do anyway in the form of action figure keychain dolls of the Governator himself. You should make a "World's Strongest Man" board game, complete with two dice, rope, weights, hernia belt, and an RV that the players would have to tow. It's a game I think I'd win thumbs down.

I'm writing you now to give you plenty of development time for its Christmas release date (hopefully). I can't wait to play your new game.

Thank you,

Jarod Kintz

4

Dear Fossil,

Do you think dinosaurs wore watches? If so, maybe they knew when their time was up.

I don't wear a watch myself, because I don't believe in time, or rather I choose not to acknowledge it. That way, when Armageddon comes, maybe I'll be spared.

You know how they make nonalcoholic beer? Could you sell me a dysfunctional watch, so I could still look stylish, yet retain my ignorance? I don't want a broken watch, because that is not new and perfect. I want a watch that was intentionally designed not to work.

I hope you can accommodate my needs and you respond in a timely matter. But if you don't, it's not like I would know how long it took you to write back.

Sincerely,

Jarod Kintz

15

Dear eBay,

I love the concept of an online auction, but last time I sold something on eBay, I broke my keyboard because I slammed my mallet too hard into it at the closing of the sale.

It always amazes me what prices people will pay for some of the crap I sell. I mean, it's not like they can't just walk into their own neighbor's yard and scoop some up for themselves. People are way too lazy today. They'd rather have the poop shipped to them, rather than bend down and apply a little effort.

Anyway, I just wanted to say thanks for providing this unique business/consumer dynamic in the marketplace.

Sincerely,

Jarod Kintz

23

Dear Bridgestone,

The world is about balance, much like a good set of tires. Good and evil are the major balancing forces in this realm we call life.

I think the most evil invention in the history of mankind has to be brakes, because I feel the greatest, most noble invention in the history of man is the wheel. Brakes are jealous of the wheel's majesty, they only serve to slow the wheel down, and they are always trying to wear the wheel down and make them stop doing what they do best.

What they do best is rotate, and nature appreciates this. The earth rotates, the seasons rotate, and my hips rotate when I gyrate them. So you guys keep on making great tires, and don't let those brake manufacturers slow you down.

Best,

Jarod Kintz

19,

Dear Sony,

Thinking about all of your electronics makes me smile brighter than a Philips flat screen TV. Of course, I don't really have an electric smile, because if I did, every time I drank something, I'd electrocute myself.

Being electrocuted runs in the family. My aunt was electrocuted the morning she realized she had no hot water in the shower, so she decided to get warm by bringing in her electric blanket. And then my snappy grandpappy Willard died in the electric chair—not the ones used in prisons, but this was an actual chair that plugs into the wall. And somebody decided to duct tape him to that chair, plug it into the wall, and throw both him and the chair into the pool. I was devastated for about a week after he died because we had to have the pool drained and I couldn't go swimming.

You can see that electronics are a big part of my heritage. If you ever need a consumer to be a part of any of your test market surveys, I'd be more than happy to give you my neighbors' phone number. They are always doing random things like that. Well, I'll talk to you later.

Sincerely,

Jarod Kintz

8

Dear Rooms To Go,

If there were no instruments and no voices in the world, would man's ears be merely for decoration?

Ears are funny-looking when you take them as stand-alone objects—they are not aesthetically fit for decoration. I'd much rather decorate my house with the olfactory in mind. Nobody would come to my place and say the walls have ears—they'd say the walls have noses. Every room in my house would have a nasal theme, except the bathroom of course.

I believe life is like being on a unicycle on a tightrope—it's all about balance. Life and death, black and white, yin and yang. What is the opposite and complimentary anatomical object of the human nose? The index finger, that's what. How much would it cost to decorate my entire two-bedroom apartment in noses and fingers? Can we do it for under twenty thousand dollars? I look forward to your reply.

Thank you,

Jarod Kintz

5

Dear Oakbrook Walk,

I don't know if you've heard the exciting news yet, but I'll be moving back down to Gainesville in less than four months. And I am hoping to lease a two-bedroom apartment with my friend and business partner, Mr. Fizzlebush.

We own our own company, Beach Bathrooms. It's based on a simple concept, really. Everyone likes to go to the bathroom in the sea, but not everybody has access to the world's largest toilet, also known as the ocean. So we bring that pure elation that accompanies going to the bathroom at the beach to all landlocked people. It's basically nothing more than sand and a box, but it greatly conserves on people's water bills.

I know what you're thinking: "Hey, that sounds a lot like a litter box. And litter boxes mean pets, and we don't allow pets here at Oakbrook Walk." Well yes, it basically is like a litter box, but what does the term "pet" mean anyway? We at Beach Bathrooms believe that a pet is anyone or anything that you love enough to scoop their excrement out of a tiny box every morning. And I guess that makes each and every one of my customers his or her own pet. (My grandma is our only customer so far. We talked her into trading in her old bed pan for our newest model that's shaped like a kitchen sink, for all those culinary types.)

So I'm hoping you won't consider me to be my own pet, and allow Mr. Fizzlebush and I to move in at the end of the summer.

Thank you,

Jarod Kintz

14

Dear ShowDog.com,

I've always wanted to be a professional dog walker, but I'm just not good on all fours. And my Mr. Fizzlebush moves more like a bear than a cat, but he only eats dog food and he only dates women who speak English as a second language.

English is not his native tongue—his is a bit rougher and much more pink. We both want to be professional dog walkers, but neither one of us know the first thing about modeling. I've heard of models learning how to walk the catwalk, but where does one go to learn how to dog walk? I feel that I could be the poster child for urban canine clothing, and I can hardly wait for your reply.

Thank you,

Jarod Kintz

5

Dear Frito-Lay,

I like your chips so much that sometimes I wish everything I owned were made out of your chips—except my shoes, because I don't like crushed chips as much as whole chips. And also not Mr. Fizzlebush either, because his fur is soft and silky and your chips are coarse and rough.

But maybe Mr. Fizzlebush's tongue could be a Frito-Lay chip, because it already is coarse and rough and then when he licks my plate of food, I wouldn't mind eating it afterwards.

But the real reason I am writing to you today is I think you guys need to relocate to Silicon Valley. You guys need to start making computer chips. I think my computer would run faster if I dumped a bag of your chips onto the motherboard. And indeed that's what I did, but I think that the dip I dumped on later fried some of the circuits.

You could make the world's first edible computer, or just the computer chips. I'd love to go to a gas station and buy a bag of computer chips. No longer would people die of heart attacks—they'd die because their stomachs got so smart, they took over their bodies only to have a mutiny of the other body parts out of intellectual jealousy. The stomach, along with the rest of everyone's bodies, would starve to death.

This is exciting! I anxiously look forward to seeing a new Frito-Lay computer, or just the computer chips, on the market soon.

Best,

Jarod Kintz

22

Dear Hunt's,

Blood may be thicker than water, but it's certainly not as thick as ketchup. Nor does it go as well with French fries.

I once tried to stab my brother with a French fry, but he was too cunning for that. He deftly jumped out of the way and countered with a juicy pickle. You can never fully appreciate life until you've stared death in its slimy, green eye.

I'm writing to ask your opinion of the following: If the Red Sea were made of ketchup when Moses parted it, what would the outcome have been if the Egyptians all got off their chariots/hot dog vending carts and took the time to enjoy the condiment? How would this single event have changed the street-vending history of the world?

I look forward to your reply. In the meantime, keep on making the world's finest ketchup.

Thank you,

Jarod Kintz

5

Dear Bellagio,

Everywhere I go, people assume I'm from Las Vegas. And it's not entirely because I dress and do my hair like Elvis, or drive a pink Cadillac. No, I'm not an impersonator of his—I've just inherited a natural style and sex appeal from nature, and a pink Cadillac from my grandmother.

But the main reason I exude a Vegas demeanor is because I'm a compulsive gambler. I bet on anything and everything—things like if it's going to rain tomorrow, what time if it does, and will anybody be run over by a bus tonight? You know, the odds go up greatly that somebody will get hit if you're driving the bus.

Well, I am driving the bus—all the way to Vegas, baby. And I hope to stay at your hotel. But since there are so many fraudulent people in Vegas who look like me, I'll be doing a complete makeover of my appearance just for the trip. I'll be dressed like Jack Nicholson doing a Robert Downey Jr. impression of Whoopi Goldberg. Basically, I'll look like a vagrant, a homeless person.

But to get to the point of this e-mail, I'm wondering how much it will cost to book a bench of yours for the weekend, taking into account the fact that I'll be bringing my own newspapers to sleep with? I look forward to your reply.

Best,

Jarod Kintz

18

Dear Arby's,

For the past year, I've been trying to set a world record. After thousands of broken plates, rejection letters, bowling-ball-related injuries, and many other fiascos, I think I may have that perfect idea. But I'll need your help to achieve it.

Together, I'd like to design and build the world's largest combination suspension bridge and roast beef sandwich. By the time of its completion in the year 2020, it will span from New York City to London, England. We'll also need to partner up with Ziploc to ensure that our bridge doesn't start to rot over the course of many hot summers.

This should not only bring you fantastic publicity, but it will also bring me my much-coveted Guinness world record. With your go-ahead, I'd like to start building after my nap tomorrow afternoon.

Thank you,

Jarod Kintz

12

Dear Orville Redenbacher's,

Popcorn always makes me think of my youth. Mother used to make us pack popcorn when we would take really long trips. That way, when the U.S. mailmen threw around the boxes we were traveling in, we didn't break that many bones.

I used to love being surrounded by popcorn, so much that sometimes I even wished I could be some popcorn. But then I reconsidered because I don't like being shoved in the microwave too much.

Those are some of my least favorite childhood memories. Good thing I didn't have my braces on during the times I spent in the microwave. I now have a phobia of microwaves, so sadly I haven't been able to pop any of your wonderful popcorn in years. Is there any way I can pop your bags of popcorn without using the microwave?

Frightfully yours,

Jarod Kintz

5

Dear Purina,

I've heard it said that Taco Bell's meat is the same quality as dog food, but I've never made a burrito out of dog food that tasted as great as one from Taco Bell. Do you sell higher-end dog food that I might be able to make a better burrito out of?

On a separate note, they say that dogs are man's best friend. Do you think that a creature who was half-man, half-dog would be the loneliest being, because he was his own best friend, or the happiest being? I hope to hear back from you soon on the high-end beef.

Thank you,

Jarod Kintz

1

Dear Julliard,

It must be wonderful to be as musical as you are. I'm not at all musical. Even if I had ears for eyes, I still couldn't read music. If I had that, I'd be blind as a bat, but I'd be Beethoven.

My cousin's a musical prodigy. He's also blind as a bat, and he lives in a cave where he orchestrates his masterpieces. He works a lot with echoes, as well as strange screeching noises. He explained his musical theory to me, but I must confess it was over my head (and not just because he was hanging upside down from the cave ceiling, either).

He's basically a mixture of Batman and Beethoven. He's Beethman! You definitely need to recruit him for your school. He could revolutionize music as we know it. If you need to get in touch with him, I'll show you which cave he dwells in. I look forward to hearing back from you soon.

Thank you,

Jarod Kintz

4

Dear Cingular,

If a man with multiple personality disorder has two pairs of ears, four arms, four mouths, and four Cingular phones, he could, under your friends and family plan, talk to himself all day long for free, couldn't he?

I'm not asking for myself—I'm asking for a friend of mine. What? Oh, right, a friend of ours. Yes, that does include you, Jimmy. Sorry, I'm back. We look forward to hearing from you soon about our, I mean my, question.

Thank you,

Jarod Kintz & friends

19,

Dear eBirdseed.com,

It's been said that a man trapped in his own mind is not a man, he's an animal. Do you know who said that? My nephew, just before he went crazy in his isolated cell. After that, most of us, Uncle Tabitha aside, felt really awful about having him committed in the asylum. Aside from his breath, that smelled like the cream cheese I used to keep in my gym socks in middle school, and his odd habit of wearing his underwear on the outside of his sweaters, he really wasn't all that bad.

He was a ventriloquist by trade, and he used to scream at his mother, my sister, and make it look like I was yelling at her—which I always found odd, because I'm a mime by profession, even though I'm quite unprofessional. But he's doing better now that he lost his voice, his job, and his entire collection of Scooby Doo paraphernalia, and he is now living comfortably in the bushes in our backyard. He bathes occasionally in the bird feeder, and we feed him bird seed everyday.

But I am writing to you today because I am wondering how much bird seed should you normally feed an abnormal, or just plain crazy, man? I look forward to your response soon.

Thank you,

Jarod Kintz

8

Dear Best Buy,

What does it mean to be the best? It means you have to be better than the number two guy. But what gratification is there in that? He's a loser—that's why he's number two. You have to be better than the best.

That's why I think you guys should change your name to Better Than Best Buy. Let everybody know you're not just the best, you're better than the best. This is an old-woman-on-the-edge-of-the-stairs-kind of marketing campaign—all you need is a good push to make a killing. Let me know if you decide to use my idea.

Best, or Better Than Best,

Jarod Kintz

5

Dear Louis Vuitton,

Hello, my name is Jarod Kintz, but you can call me Jarod. Do you mind if I call you Lou? How about Big Lou?

Big Lou, I've always been into women's purses, usually while they weren't looking, so it seems only natural now that I should want to design them. Working together, me and you, Big Lou, I hope to design the world's largest purse. It will be roughly the size and shape of a Boeing 747, except it will have your logo across the wings and fin. And on the promotional first flight, the only people allowed on the plane will have to come dressed in costume as giant Louis Vuitton wallets.

You may be thinking, who is the target market for one of these "super purses," as I like to call them? Well, Elton John, for one. And the best part is, unless Lockheed Martin goes into the black market, this will be your least-bootlegged purse ever. I don't know about you, but I don't see too many street vendors hawking fake Delta planes at the flea markets.

I hope you see the value of developing a super purse, and I look forward to doing business with you.

Thank you,

Jarod Kintz

1

Dear Wonder Bread,

You are such a wonderful corporation that I think you should have a picnic for all your employees and a few privileged customers (wink, wink, quack, quack).

Just in case you decide to hold the picnic, I am RSVPing right now, and I will be attending dressed as a giant duck. It would be marvelously fun if you could throw me chunks of your delicious bread as I snap them up with my beak. But, please, only throw bread. At the last company picnic I attended, some of the crueler corporate executives took to throwing heavier things at me such as hot dogs, whole watermelons, and even a few trombones. (It was a music retailers' picnic.)

I look forward to a full day of fun, and a stomach full of soggy bread.

Yours Truly,

Jarod Kintz

12

Dear Vision Works,

If I had an eyeball on each foot, would you make glasses for me that had lenses embedded in the tongue?

Well, fortunately for both of us, I don't have an eyeball on each foot. But I do have two feet growing out of my forehead. A lot of people are grossed out by feet, and they fear giving me eye contact. I was wondering if you could make me a pair of glasses that had tennis shoes attached to the frame? This way, people would be compelled, out of curiosity, to look me in the face. I hope to hear back from you soon.

Sincerely,

Jarod Kintz

23

Dear Albertsons,

You have no idea how great it feels to be writing to you right now. I just recently got the use of my fingers back.

For over six months, I was paralyzed from the wrist down. That meant I couldn't play the piano—not that I know how to play the piano, but I wanted to try it really bad while I was an eight-digit decrepit. (I lost two fingers to the Yakuza.) I also lost the ability to count, not from the fall, but because I can only count on my fingers.

Now that I have the use of my fingers back, I am writing you to encourage you to lobby the food manufacturers to switch from the metric system, which uses a base-ten system, to my new "eccentric system," which uses a base-eight. This would make measurements drastically easier for everybody who is operating in life with only eight fingers. Also, is it just me, or do you also think that the week should have eight days, and not seven days in it? The extra day could be used for fishing or playing the piano, or rest, or whatever—a second Sabbath, perhaps.

I look forward to hearing what your inquiries on the switch of major manufacturers to a base-eight system may lead to.

Thank you,

Jarod Kintz

1

Dear Yankee Candle Company,

If there were a candle the size and shape of the Empire State Building, and it burned down, do you think the people of New York City would drown in wax?

I would rather burn alive than live life as a candle. But if I was one of your candles I wouldn't need to wear deodorant because I'd always smell great. And I'd finally be welcome in a woman's bedroom. Women would finally find me romantic. When I was growing up, other boys wanted to be policemen and firemen. Not me—I always wanted to be a candle. But after I burned down my second house in six months, mother made me change my aspirations.

Now I work with the homeless. That's right, I'm unemployed. When you're homeless, there is always an abundance of time, and never enough money to burn. (I still like burning things.) Well, I gotta skedaddle—the fire department will be here at any moment.

Take care,

Jarod Kintz

25

Dear Saturn,

Your car is out of this world. Three planets over, to be exact.

Sometimes I wish I could drive your car around the sun. I'd probably need lots of sunscreen though. (I burn easily. Just ask my friends, who turned the oven on when they discovered I was hiding there during last week's game of hide-n-seek.)

I think you guys should create a super SUV called "The Comet." Then it would be socially acceptable to crash into random things and places here on Earth. Let me know what you think of my new concept car.

Sincerely,

Jarod Kintz

19

Dear Denny's,

Your food is delicious! Every time I eat there, I never feel like vomiting afterwards, although I force myself to anyway.

It's not because I'm a Communist, which I'm not, but I'm not a Communist only because I abhor the color red. I'd also rather not share a meal with a socialist if I had the option of dining alone or with a capitalist.

Mr. Fizzlebush is a capitalist, but only because he is afraid of Karl Marx's beard and stern look. He is also afraid of tall hats, which means that every Halloween, I dress up like Abe Lincoln and scare the you-know-what out of him. And he always does his business right on my favorite rug, too. And it's usually big business—that's how I know he's a capitalist.

But to my point. I will be dining at your establishment this Thursday the 23rd, and I will be bringing Mr. Fizzlebush. I was wondering if you could have all your servers, both male and female, at your Gainesville location, dress like Abe Lincoln? It will be great! Mr. Fizzlebush's fear is so great that I've owed him five dollars for the past year over a bet on who the first president of the U.S was. (I know it is inconsequential, as life in general is, but how was I to know that Jean-Paul Sartre was not a president, let alone even an American?). So I've owed him this five-dollar bill this whole time, yet he won't take it because Abe's image is on there.

I hope you decide to comply with this prank, and I promise to tip well. (I'm dying to get rid of this five-dollar bill.) If you don't respond, I'll assume by your silence that you are going into stealth mode for this prank so that Mr. Fizzlebush doesn't find out. I look forward to next Thursday.

Thank you,

Jarod Kintz

6

Dear Hershey's,

I am a total outdoorsy kind of guy. I'm also a certified chocolate fiend.

Whenever I'm in the woods, I think about those unfortunate people who, for whatever reason, are forced to cut off one of their limbs to survive. Then I think, hey, how cool would it be if one of their arms were made of chocolate? Then not only would they be able to free themselves, but they'd also have a delicious reward for being so brave.

Are you planning on branching out into the prosthetic limb industry anytime soon? I'd love to eat my own elbow, especially if it was made of milk chocolate and had chunks of nuts in it. Even if you don't reply, I'll still continue to buy your candy bars.

Best of luck,

Jarod Kintz

15

Dear U-Haul,

How many goats can you typically fit in your largest moving van? Why do the seats of your vans smell like burnt cheese?

Back when my family first moved to this country, there was not enough cheese to go around—nor goats, but one goat could have been shared among five grown men, each taking their turn in descending order of age. (It gets cold and lonely in Wyoming.)

I wish clothes were made of cheese, and shoes were made of bread. That way if I were stuck in the desert, I could still have a grilled cheese sandwich. And moving would be easy—all I'd need would be the cheese on my back. Of course, I don't like moldy clothes, so I wouldn't have a dresser, but rather, a refrigerator.

I am thinking of moving to Wisconsin. I have about a half-ton of cheddar cheese to move. Are your vans refrigerated? I depart as soon as you reply.

Thank you,

Jarod Kintz

12

Dear American Society of Plastic Surgeons,

My girlfriend wants to get breast implants, but I'm not sure if I'd like that.

She tells me they'd cost around $8,000. I was wondering if her new breasts would also come with a steering wheel? Because if I'm paying that kind of money for something, I at least want to be able to drive it around.

Also, she sleeps on her stomach, so I was wondering if we got the operation, could we put the breasts on her back, so I could have something to play with while she's asleep?

And finally, do you know where I can get it done at discount prices? Maybe buy one breast, get the second one half-off. I look forward to hearing back from you.

Thank you,

Jarod Kintz

12

Dear Oscar Mayer,

Sometimes I think my girlfriend has bologna for brains. So every time we get into a screaming argument, I always squirt her in the face with mustard.

She says that's abuse, and I think she's right. No mustard, Dijon included, should be subjected to that kind of treatment. Sometimes I feel cornered in this relationship, like I'm trapped between a piece of tomato and a crisp of lettuce. Since you are the masters of the meat, what can I do to deal with my girlfriend and all her b.s. (bologna sandwich)? I desperately await your reply.

Sincerely,

Jarod Kintz

15

Dear Toastmasters,

Nobody loves toast as much as I do, with the possible exception of Mr. Fizzlebush and Missy Bisquik. Oh, and Baby Spartacus, and maybe Gunther Girl. But besides them, I am the ultimate fan of toast.

Yet, you guys claim to be the masters of toast. I can spread a stick of butter evenly across a piece of toast the size of Texas. And you can't prove I can't, unless you have a piece of toast the size of Texas. And Texas toast doesn't count either.

I think we need to have a toast-off. Let's see who can cook and consume the most toast within a ten-minute timeframe. And you can't bring in a ringer, while I promise I won't enlist the help of Mr. Fizzlebush. Toast is, was, and will always be the breakfast of champions. Unless you have no elbows, you know how to reach me.

Best,

Jarod Kintz

23

Dear Gillette,

If Mt. Rushmore had facial hair, and I were to shave the presidents' faces using one of your razors, by the time I finished with the fourth President's face, the President I started with would have a full beard again—unless you made a jumbo razor.

Do you make jumbo razors for giants and people of great stature? What about mini-razors for people of not-so-great stature? Well I've got to go shave my Choch now. (Choch is my curly-haired cat.)

Toodles,

Jarod Kintz

19

Dear Crest,

You guys make the best sports drink ever! Just one tube can really quench my thirst after a long run. And I can roll it up and stuff it in my shoe while I run also. It's truly the first space-age sports drink.

And it's not even completely liquid! If being a liquid were heterosexuality, your sports drink would be more ambiguous than Oscar Wilde. It's more of a sports gel, but it tastes great. All the top athletes should drink Crest before, during, and after any major sporting event.

Thank you,

Jarod Kintz

20

Dear eMachines,

Do you remember the cartoon *He-Man*? I think you guys should have a mascot called, eMan. And instead of Skeletor, your arch enemy could be Delletor. The e-pic battle of electronic men would be great for consumers everywhere.

Instead of the sword that He-Man wielded, you guys could throw hard drives at each other. If you need someone to illustrate the cartoon for you, just let me know. I'll be more than happy to decline your offer.

Thank you,

Jarod Kintz

8

Dear Powerade,

This past month has been the lowest point in my life. My best friend, Charles Manseur Fizzlebush Grissham III, ran away with my girlfriend. On top of that heartache, my grandmother died. With her passing, I inherited her sizeable panty collection accumulated over nearly eighty years. (I was her favorite grandson.)

These two events were such a shock to me that I've been sitting here for weeks, wearing her panties, eating cat food, and chugging Powerade—but I still feel powerless. I know I shouldn't feel this way after such treachery, but I miss Mr. Fizzlebush and I want him back. Do you guys make a super Powerade for the emotionally drained? If not, I guess I'll continue to sit here, drinking my Powerade and hoping to regain my strength.

Yours truly,

Jarod Kintz

5

Dear Farmer's Almanac,

I know that there are 365 days in a year, and also 52 weeks in a year. But if you do the math, 52 weeks is only 364 days. What happened to that extra day? Is that day a Tuesday? Because that's when Mr. Fizzlebush went missing.

He disappeared over the Bermuda Triangle en route to Miami from Tampa. Don't ask me how that worked out. Do you think that missing day every year is also in the Bermuda Triangle? Do you know if that missing day counts as one of my vacation days at work? If it does, I'm sure not going on vacation anywhere near the Bermuda Triangle.

Maybe I'll plan a vacation for my father-in-law to leave out of Miami International on that day and hope I never have to listen to any more of his jokes about cats. (Mr. Fizzlebush is/was a cat.) Well, I hope you can solve this mystery for me.

Thank you,

Jarod Kintz

13

Dear Doublemint Gum,

Sometimes I wish I had five mouths, one for each piece in a pack of your gum. But I don't have five mouths, I only have two. (I was conceived at a radioactive waste site.) So I can only eat two at a time without stuffing my mouth.

Sometimes my ear pops (I only have one) when I chew gum. I like smacking my gum while having conversations with strange people on the public transportation system. Because of my birth defect, I generally talk about twice as much as I listen. And my brother talks with his hands, so he talks about three times as much as he listens. He has no mouth though, so he chews your gum with his feet (which does nothing to improve his breath).

I would say that I like your gum about double (that's nearly twice) as much as your average customer. Doublemint is all about doubling your pleasure, right? Well, I'm DoubleMouth Man (that's my superhero name), and I think once TV viewers got over the initial shock of my abnormalities, I'd be a hit. I'd be the smack of the town, or at least Doublemint would be, as more people rushed to the stores to buy what I told them to buy. (Of course, I wouldn't be speaking out of both sides of both of my mouths, because I really do love your product.)

Just a thought for you to chew on, but don't swallow it (it might take seven years to digest), and get back to me.

Thank you,

Jarod Kintz

1

Dear P.F. Chang's,

Your egg rolls are splendid, like staring into the sun with frozen retinas, except without the cheese melted on my eyelids from too much time in the microwave.

Your egg drop soup is as if Jesus himself was cross-country skiing on cirrus clouds, except without the sandals in my soup. How I love dining at your establishment. I'd much rather do that than shave my testicles and superglue them to the trailer hitch of an Iowan family bound for Orlando on vacation.

Best,

Jarod Kintz

4

Dear Kenny G,

You woo me with your music whenever I hear it. I think you are the world's greatest flutist, despite the fact that you play the saxophone. Most people couldn't make that distinction, but I have a keen ear for music. I keep the musical ear in a jar in the basement. If you ever see it, it's enough to make you lose your lunch. But then so is bad sax.

Kenneth, do you mind if I call you Kenneth? Kenneth, if it weren't for your music, I don't know how I'd ever fall asleep at night. I look forward to seeing you when you come into Jacksonville next.

Sincerely,

Jarod Kintz

14

Dear Atlanta Bread Company,

I'd like to buy a custom loaf of bread, but I do not live in Atlanta. I live in Florida. Can we still do business?

The loaf I want to buy will be whole wheat, and stretch from Seattle to Dallas. (I am attempting a world record for the longest sandwich ever made.) Do you charge by the foot, the mile, or the calorie?

In your expert opinion, what is the most efficient way to spread mayonnaise over such a great distance? I think ten thousand people, each with a butter knife, would be slightly quicker than one person with ten thousand butter knives, but I still have to test that in my lab (grandmother's kitchen). Also, do you think that the meat I place in the sandwich in Dallas will be spoiled by the time the last slice of ham is laid down in Seattle? I guess it really doesn't matter, since I am giving it away to homeless people after I'm done.

I look forward to your reply, and to conducting business with you.

Sincerely,

Jarod Kintz

5

Dear Verizon,

I just got my phone bill today, and I am very upset. Why am I getting charged ten cents per text message? And if my nights start at 8:00, can I call California for free, or do I have to wait for their nights to start?

I hear you have great customer service, so I hope I'm not wasting my time in writing to you. I think it's about time to get out of my Cingular contract and switch to AT&T. What do you think? If you could answer these questions for me, I'd be very grateful.

Thanks,

Jarod Kintz

19

Dear Google,

Isn't a googol synonymous with ten duotrigintillion? And isn't a googol a numeral one with a hundred zeros after it? Is that how much money you guys have? If so, you guys must pay some exorbitant taxes.

I try not to pay taxes myself. I can do that because I don't use money. If I want to buy something, like a car for example, I might offer the salesman a hundred goats, fourteen grilled cheese sandwiches, or an exclusive autographed picture of myself in compromising situations.

Are you guys hiring by any chance? I know a little about computers. You'd have to pay me a salary of at least forty horses a year, or seventy-five llamas (their value is really inflated in South America). I don't have an official resume, but I've been a shepherd for nine years now, and my record with sexual activity among the flock is nearly flawless. I hope you guys hire me soon. I need the livestock.

Thank you,

Jarod Kintz

19.

Dear Pacific Lumber Company,

Hello, my name is Jarod, and I live in a tree fort in my grandmother's yard. I also live in constant fear that one day you will show up at my bottom step with a chainsaw demanding to cut down my home.

But I'd rather you cut my left arm off. (Don't worry, I'm right handed.) Or even better, I'd rather have you cut off one of my girlfriend's legs so she knows what it feels like to lean on someone. She's so damned independent! She refuses to sleep at my place—she says she's afraid of termites. That's almost as absurd as a lumberjack who's afraid of wood.

Hey, here's a thought: what if that same lumber-fearing lumberjack were also afraid of horses? Well, he wouldn't have made a very good Trojan, that's for sure. Being a lumberjack, I'm sure you know what it feels like to urinate from a tree branch thirty feet in the air. My aim is so good now that I can pee in a milk carton without it even touching the lip of the container. But grandmother doesn't like it when I do that. She says it makes the milk taste funny.

Well, I gotta go, I think I hear my grandmother hollering at me. (I hope I don't get a whipping. I think she suspects it's me who's been soiling her rugs and NOT Mr. Fizzlebush, her cat.) So please don't cut down my tree fort. I really don't want to move back into grandmother's basement. It smells like a mixture of mothballs and cat piss down there.

Thank you,

Jarod Kintz

-10.

Dear FedEx,

You know that phrase, "You've got to start somewhere, might as well start in the mailroom and work your way up?" Yeah, well that might apply in your company, but since you guys are so big now, and have so many customers, it doesn't apply in the job I want. They don't have a mailroom.

Oh, I'm so confused! If there is no mailroom, no bottom, then there's only a middle and a top. And I can't start in the middle of a company. That's like running a marathon and starting on mile eight—I'd get disqualified. So I guess I'm asking your advice with how to proceed with my career. Confucius never said, "A journey of a thousand miles starts with the 5,000th step." Please respond quickly. I am in desperate need of your counsel.

Thank you,

Jarod Kintz

15.

Dear Dillard's,

Let me first start out by saying that I, Jarod Kintz, am your store's biggest fan. Not in size (I am only four feet eleven), but in spirit and shopping habits.

As much as I love your store, I feel that there is one thing missing: handicapped mannequins. While I myself am not crippled, I feel there is a serious shortage of paralyzed models. The handicapped are just underrepresented in the fashion world. They have to buy clothes, too. It would be a beautiful thing to see a mannequin in a wheelchair for all those paralyzed patrons of yours. I look forward to hearing back from you about this proposal of mine.

Thank you,

Jarod Kintz

11

Dear Napa Auto Parts,

I just got off the phone with The Home Depot, and they are going to help me build a stand-alone garage outside of my house that's in the shape of a giant car. Now I've got to build a custom car that looks like a garage to park in it. Do you guys have the necessary parts to do that, or would you have to custom fabricate them?

Also, do you sell giant bumpers that I can attach to my new garage? And do you know if I have to have a valid license to drive a garage? What about if I just park it? Also, do I need proof of insurance on my garage, since it will look like a car? Any helpful information you could give me would be most helpful.

Thank you,

Jarod Kintz

9

Dear Trojan,

I am writing to you today under great duress, because tomorrow is my twenty-fourth birthday. This is good news because, while I haven't yet been with a woman, mother keeps reassuring me, and telling me that the day is near.

So I went to the store to buy some prophylactics, and I saw both regular and Magnum. But I was wondering if you carried extra-small? (I'd probably like my condoms like my jeans—baggy.) I need a response really quick, because I really don't want to resort to using Saran Wrap (mother needs it for the casserole). I look forward to your reply.

Sincerely,

Jarod Kintz

14

Dear U.S. Army,

I really appreciate all you are doing for the safety of America and for the rest of the world.

I have noticed that when I watch a TV recruiting commercial that all of the soldiers seem to be men. I have a suggestion that would make women enlist in the Army. Instead of your ad campaign that says, an "Army of One," you should change it to "Girls Gun Wild." And you could show a bunch of beautiful women in bikinis shooting machine guns. I have a strong hunch that girls would flock, like vultures over a festering corpse, to join the Army.

What do you think of this marketing strategy? I look forward to hearing from you.

Thank you,

Jarod Kintz

PS: Would you be needing my excellent fighting skills? I haven't been in too many fights, but I was a ballerina for several weeks. I have strong calf muscles. I'm thinking Green Beret. But you have to pay me more, seeing as how I am sort of a ringer for you guys. Let me know, you have my number. But don't call after nine—mother doesn't like it.

20

Dear Gatorade,

I understand that you were created at the University of Florida. That's crazy, because I'm a UF dropout. Well, I actually transferred to FSU (bad move, I know), but I plan on going back to graduate.

My question for you is, if all the oceans in the world were filled with Gatorade, and not seawater, do you think more homeless people would sleep on the beach? And then by consuming all the free Gatorade, would we have a new breed of athlete? I just can't imagine how bad a homeless locker room would smell after a sweaty game. I hope you take the time to carefully consider my question and get back to me.

Thanks,

Jarod Kintz

26

Dear Ted Nancy,

Ever since papyrus and the pen were invented, people have been writing prank notes and letters. Then the telephone came, and people had the luxury of making voice contact with random people and pretending to be anybody, all within the comfort of their grandmother's living room while wearing her panties. (It's better to do this when she's not home).

Then in the late twentieth century, your book came out, and it was clear that you had taken pranks to the next level. Most people who read your book were inspired to laugh and tell their friends. But I was inspired to do more. Your letters are the single reason I decided to write a book. So I wrote a few prank e-mails in December of 2004, then decided to write a short humor novel instead. Then here recently, I decided to pick back up with the e-mails.

Now it's true that this e-mail here I did not actually send to you because I don't have your e-mail address. But I felt compelled to write something to you to let you know that I appreciated your humor, and that I think you are a comic genius.

Your loyal fan,

Jarod Kintz

978-0-595-39721-1
0-595-39721-2